LUCY THE ~~BAD~~ GOOD

LUCY
THE
BAD GOOD

Marianne Musgrove

illustrated by
Cheryl Orsini

Henry Holt and Company ⭐ New York

Henry Holt and Company, LLC
Publishers since 1866
175 Fifth Avenue
New York, New York 10010
www.HenryHoltKids.com

Henry Holt® is a registered trademark of Henry Holt and Company, LLC.
Text copyright © 2008 by Marianne Musgrove
Illustrations copyright © 2008 by Cheryl Orsini
First published in the United States in 2010 by Henry Holt and Company, LLC
Originally published in Australia in 2008 by Random House Australia
All rights reserved.
Distributed in Canada by H. B. Fenn and Company Ltd.

Library of Congress Cataloging-in-Publication Data
Musgrove, Marianne.
Lucy the good / Marianne Musgrove; illustrated by Cheryl Orsini. — 1st American ed.
p.   cm.
Summary: When Lucy's great-aunt Bep comes from Holland to Adelaide,
Australia, to visit, she is shocked by some of Lucy's behavior, and Lucy begins to
wonder about herself. Includes a glossary of Dutch words and a recipe.
ISBN 978-0-8050-9051-2
[1. Behavior—Fiction. 2. Self-perception—Fiction. 3. Great-aunts—Fiction.
4. Schools—Fiction. 5. Family life—Australia—Fiction. 6. Dutch—Australia—
Fiction. 7. Australia—Fiction.] I. Orsini, Cheryl, ill. II. Title.
PZ7.M9693Lu 2010   [Fic]—dc22 2009050766

First American Edition—2010 / Designed by Véronique Lefèvre Sweet
Printed in August 2010 in the United States of America
by R. R. Donnelly & Sons Company, Harrisonburg, Virginia

1 3 5 7 9 10 8 6 4 2

*In memory of Dad: the trips to the museum,
bush walks in the Gorge, our special rock, the
bagatelles and Chocolate Night, Channel Two,
the Alhambra and that terry-toweling hat.*

# CHAPTER ONE

Tantrum, wrote Lucy, sounding out the word in her head so she could spell it right: *t–a–n–tr–um.*

I must not throw a temper tantrum in class.

Unless absolutely necessary, she added to herself. Like today. There had been a perfectly good reason why she had emptied Jacinta's pencil case all over the floor.

Lucy was in the Time Out chair now. She was supposed to look straight ahead, but she turned when she heard her teacher talking to Jacinta.

"And what's your poem about?" said Ms. Denny.

"A unicorn," Jacinta replied.

"Nice work, Jacinta," said Ms. Denny. "Good girl."

"I wrote it all by myself. Not like some people."
Jacinta looked over at Lucy and smiled a smile that
grown-ups think is a friendly smile but kids know
really means, "Ha, ha, ha. You're in the Time Out
chair and I'm not."

Lucy gave Jacinta her best squinty-eyed look of
hate, then turned to face the wall again. She imagined she and Jacinta were on a boat. A storm was

coming. Jacinta had fallen overboard and Lucy was the only one who knew she was in the water. She was the only one who could throw her a life jacket.

"Please, Lucy!" cried Jacinta. "Please throw me a life jacket!"

"Well, I don't know...," said Lucy, imagining herself holding the jacket just out of Jacinta's reach. "Are you going to tell the truth?"

"The truth about what?" said Jacinta.

"The truth about my poem."

That morning, Ms. Denny had asked everyone to write a poem about their favorite animal. Lucy had chosen a two-humped camel, the same as her favorite toy, Nathan.

Writing poems was something Lucy was good at. She had worked hard on her camel poem all morning, doing lots of crossing out and rewriting.

When she was finished, Ms. Denny asked Lucy to read it out loud in front of the whole class. Lucy did so in her best speaking voice, and everyone clapped at the end. Then Ms. Denny gave her a pepper-mint from the tin on her desk. Ms. Denny only ever gave out peppermints for the very best poems.

Later, while their teacher handed out some work sheets, Jacinta leaned over and whispered, "You copied that poem."

"What?" said Lucy.

"I've read it before," said Jacinta. "In a magazine. You didn't make it up. You copied it."

Some of the other kids murmured their disapproval. The back-row boys, Paolo, Blake, and Girang, jeered. Lucy turned around and stuck her tongue out. She had a very long tongue that could touch the tip of her nose. She waggled it in the boys' direction. Paolo pushed his lips together with his fingers and did his frog face.

"Lucy," said Ms. Denny, "face the front, please. No bad behavior."

Jacinta waited till Ms. Denny was farther away,

then whispered, "Everyone knows you're a copier, so why don't you just admit it?"

"I am not!" hissed Lucy. "Take it back."

She pushed her peppermint to the corner of her desk. She didn't feel like eating it now. She wouldn't enjoy it properly.

"Copier," repeated Jacinta.

Lucy turned to her best friend, Harriet, for support. As usual, Harriet was sucking her long blond braid. Lucy couldn't suck her hair because it was too short. She wore it in little pigtails that stuck out on either side of her head like faucets squirting water.

"Lucy never copied," said Harriet, taking her braid out of her mouth. "So why don't you be quiet, Jacinta."

Jacinta pretended not to notice her. She doodled on her pencil case and sang softly to herself, "Lucy copied her poem. Lucy copied her poem."

"I did not," said Lucy.

"Lucy copied her poem. Lucy copied her poem," said Jacinta a little more loudly.

A couple of the other kids joined in.

"Lucy copied her poem. Lucy copied her poem."

"Settle down, class," said Ms. Denny.

The rest of the children stopped singing but not Jacinta. She looked Lucy straight in the eye and mouthed the song without making any noise. "Lucy copied her poem. Lucy copied her poem."

"I did not," said Lucy.

"Lucy copied her poem. Lucy copied her poem."

"I—did—not!"

"Lucy," warned Ms. Denny.

Jacinta smiled, still mouthing the words. Red-hot feelings rumbled inside Lucy. It was coming. Lucy knew it. Anger was pressing against her skin from the inside.

"Lucy copied her poem. Lucy copied her— Hey!"

Jacinta said the "Hey!" out loud because Lucy had gotten to her feet and grabbed Jacinta's pencil case. She tipped it upside down so that pencils decorated with tiny unicorns fell on the floor. Unicorn-shaped erasers fell out too. And unicorn stickers. They scattered all over the floor in a big mess. Lucy shook the pencil case one last time and a unicorn stamp dropped out. Lucy kicked it so hard that it skidded

6 ✫

under desks and chairs and hit the wall. Lucy hoped
it got wrecked.

"Lucy van Loon!" said Ms. Denny. "Time Out chair!
Now!"

One of the worst things about sitting in the Time Out chair was having to stare at Ms. Denny's Good Attitude Chart. It listed the names of all the students in the class. Next to each name was a space for stars. Students who had a good attitude got lots of stars. If they had a bad attitude, they didn't get any.

Lucy didn't like the word *attitude*. Her dad used it sometimes when he was mad at her. "You need to change that attitude of yours, Lucy," he would say, or, "Lucy, we don't need any of that bad attitude."

That's what he'd said that morning when he'd reminded Lucy that her great-aunt was coming to visit.

"Tante Bep's plane gets in this afternoon," he said, "and I'd like you to be on your best behavior. Do you promise to be a good girl?"

Lucy couldn't understand why Dad needed to ask. He should know she was a good girl. And anyway, Lucy and Tante Bep were going to have the

GOOD ATTITUDE CHART	
Jacinta	★★★★★
Harriet	★★★★★
Girang	★★★★
Paolo	★★★
Lucy	★

best time sharing Lucy's room and staying up late. Lucy was going to show Tante Bep all her things, and Tante Bep was going to tell Lucy stories about what it was like to live in Holland. She was even going to give Lucy a pair of Dutch wooden shoes called clogs. What was Dad worrying about?

The Good Attitude Chart had lots of names on it. Lucy's eyes rested on Jacinta's. She snorted. Eight stars already. She looked farther down the list. Harriet—five stars. Well, that made sense. Harriet always seemed to know what the school

★ 9

rules were. Even the secret ones Lucy had never heard of, such as that you shouldn't sit under the tree in the playground because that was where the tough kids played.

Lucy kept looking till she got to her own name. Lucy van Loon—one star. The only person with fewer stars was Blake, and he glued kids' faces to their desks!

One of the stars next to Jacinta's name was peeling off. *Surely she can spare one*, thought Lucy. She peeked over her shoulder to see what Ms. Denny was doing. She was busy helping Girang.

Reaching up slowly, Lucy began to peel the star. It came right off on the tip of her index finger. She checked over her shoulder again, then stuck it next to her own name. She pressed down hard with the heel of her hand. *There*, she thought. *I do have a good attitude. The chart says so.*

Still, she had only two stars. Three would be nicer. Lucy jammed her thumbnail under another of Jacinta's stars and worked away at it. When it finally came off, she pressed it next to her own name. It stuck for a moment, then curled away from the wall. Lucy licked the back of it to try to make it stick. She banged her fist over the top of it.

Without warning, the smell of peppermint wafted over her.

"What's this?" said Ms. Denny, appearing behind her. "Lucy van Loon, what are you doing?"

CHAPTER TWO

Lucy waited at the school gate for Dad. She stood on one leg, like a stork, with her eyes shut. She was trying to see how long she could last before tipping over. In her hand was a letter.

"Whatcha got there?" said Paolo.

Lucy wobbled, waved her arms around, then put her foot back down on the ground.

"You made me lose my balance," she said, opening her eyes. "I was just about to beat my record."

"Yeah, but what's that?"

Lucy looked down at the envelope. "To Mr. and Mrs. van Loon," the writing on the front said. It was

a letter from Ms. Denny about her "behavior." Lucy didn't see what all the fuss was about. After all, she was only borrowing some of Jacinta's stars. And anyway, she had a good reason. If Ms. Denny had been fair and given her lots of stars too, she wouldn't have had to do it.

"None of your business," said Lucy, stuffing the letter into her bag. "And anyway," she added, "I'm not talking to you."

"Why not?"

Lucy turned to him. "'Cause you said I copied my poem!"

"No, I didn't," said Paolo.

"You laughed," said Lucy, "and that's just as bad."

Paolo sighed. "C'mon, Lucy. We've always been friends. We're next-door neighbors, aren't we? I know you didn't copy that poem."

Lucy glanced at him skeptically. Paolo reached into his pocket, pulled something out, and pushed it into Lucy's hand. It was a squashed sandwich cookie. Lucy's favorite. Lucy knew that if she ate it, it would mean she had forgiven Paolo. She wasn't sure if she was ready to do that just yet.

"Everyone knows you're good at making up poems and stuff," said Paolo.

A tiny smile tweaked Lucy's lips. She twisted the cookie apart and looked at the circle of cream.

"Why don't you come over later?" said Paolo.

"Can't," said Lucy, taking a long, slow lick of the cream. "Dad's taking me to the airport to pick up Mum's aunt. She's visiting us from Holland."

"Can she speak English?" asked Paolo.

"She's been here in Australia for a week, visiting my uncle in Sydney," said Lucy, "so she should have got in a lot of practice."

Paolo watched Lucy as she took another long lick.

"Here," said Lucy, handing him the unlicked half. "I'll come 'round on the weekend."

Lucy's dad pulled up beside her and flung open the car door. "Quick sticks, Lucy! We're late to the airport!"

Lucy waved good-bye to Paolo, jumped in, and shut the door. She turned around to say hi to her brother, Calvin, who was in the car seat in the back. Calvin was wearing a banana costume—the costume Lucy had worn to Harriet's fruit-themed birthday party last year. She frowned at Dad.

"Don't look at me like that!" Dad said. "I've been flat-out cleaning up the place and then, just as we're about to leave, your brother decides he won't wear anything unless it's yellow. And can I find his yellow T-shirt and shorts? No. Will he wear something blue or even orange? No. So as you can see, he's wearing the only yellow thing

16 ⭐

I could find. Who knows what Tante Bep will make of us?"

Looking in the rearview mirror at the enormous banana sitting in the backseat, Lucy wondered too. She buckled up her seat belt and said, "Ready."

"Then let's go," said Dad. "We need all the green traffic lights we can get, so, kids, I need you to think of green things."

"I'm going to think of yellow things," replied Calvin.

As soon as they found a parking spot at the airport, Dad hurried them out of the car. He opened the trunk and Lucy got out the special sign she had made for Tante Bep. WELCOME TO ADELAIDE, it said. She had written the words with her red glitter glue pen and stuck smiley-face stickers around the edge.

"I'm going to walk backward the whole way," announced Calvin.

Dad watched his son walking backward between

the cars. He picked him up and hoisted him over his shoulder.

"C'mon, Lucy," he said. "Stay close!"

Dad called out more instructions while they ran. "Do you remember what we talked about, love?"

"Yeeeeees," said Lucy, trying to keep up. "I have to be good while Tante Bep is here."

"That's right," said Dad. "And not just a little bit good. A lot good, okay? I really need you to try hard for me, love."

Lucy frowned. She did try. She tried very hard.

Even when Dad wasn't looking. The problem was, things seemed to go wrong no matter what. Each morning, she would start out being good, then something would happen and the next thing you know, she was getting into trouble. Half the time, she didn't even know why. Lucy figured it was mostly other people's fault.

By the time they reached the arrival gate, most of the people had already gotten off the plane.

"Where can Tante Bep be?" said Dad, craning his neck. "Can you see any eighty-year-old women around, kids?"

"I need to do a wee," said Calvin.

"Why didn't you go when we were still at home?" said Dad.

"I didn't need to go then," said Calvin.

"You'll just have to hold on," said Dad. "Until we find Tante Bep, wherever she is. Let's try the baggage carousel."

They went back down the escalator, Calvin still slung over Dad's shoulder and Lucy close behind.

"I really need to do a wee," said Calvin. "It's a 'mergency."

Dad and Lucy looked at the baggage carousel. Tante Bep was nowhere to be seen.

"Here's what we'll do," said Dad. "We'll all go to the little boys' room and then we'll find your great-aunt."

"I'm not going in there," said Lucy.

She never went into public bathrooms if she could help it. And especially not the boys' bathrooms. At school, she held on until she got home.

"Okay, fine. The bathroom's just over there, so you stay here and don't move. We'll be back soon."

Lucy didn't mind being left alone. This was her favorite part of the airport. There was a hole in the

wall covered by heavy plastic flaps. A black conveyor belt came out of the flaps. It was called the carousel. The belt snaked around the room and back into another hole in the wall. It was a bit like a little road. Most of the time, it stood still, like now. Then, all of a sudden, it would start moving.

Suitcases would come out of the hole in the wall and people would drag them off the carousel and take them home. Lucy stepped forward to get a better look.

Imagine going for a ride on it! she thought. It would be like being at the fun fair. She put one knee on the carousel. Then she put her other knee on. Before she knew it, she had crawled right onto it. She sat down cross-legged and laid her welcome sign in front of her. *This is fun!* she thought. *I wish I could go for a real ride.*

Then the carousel started to move, curving around one corner, then another. *Woo hoo!* thought Lucy.

"Should that little girl be doing that?" someone asked.

Lucy looked away. That was when she noticed she was heading toward the other hole in the wall where the bags disappeared. *Uh-oh*, she thought. *What if I go through the hole and get mistaken for a suitcase? I might be put on a plane and sent to another country!*

"Dad!" she said, but he was still in the bathroom with Calvin.

She was moving quite fast, and the hole was getting closer. Lucy scrambled backward, trying to get away from it. Her WELCOME TO ADELAIDE sign disappeared into the hole.

"Dad!" she cried, more loudly this time.

Lucy tried to stand up, but she fell backward. She rolled onto her knees and crawled along the belt away from the hole.

"Faster!" she said to herself. "Faster!"

She continued to crawl, but now suitcases were coming toward her. Could she climb over them in time? What was she going to do?

"Help!" she cried. "Somebody, help me!"

CHAPTER THREE

Lucy was very close to being sucked into the black hole when two big hands grabbed her around the waist. The next moment, she was lifted off the baggage carousel and set down on the ground.

"That was a very naughty thing you did, little girl," said the woman who helped her off. She was wearing a big woolen cardigan even though it was warm, and she had a strong accent. "Where is your mother or father? They should be watching you."

Lucy wiped tears from her eyes. "Dad's not here," she said. "He's—"

"Lucy!" panted Dad, rushing to her side. "You poor thing!" He set down Calvin and hugged her

close. "I'm so glad you're all right. What a fright you must have had."

She certainly had had a fright! A few more tears leaked out of her eyes while Dad stroked her hair.

"You could've died," said Calvin in wonderment. "I always miss out on the good stuff."

"Are you okay?" said Dad.

"Yes," said Lucy. "No." She burst into tears again.

"It's okay," said Dad, holding her to him. "You're safe now."

When her tears had died down to a few snuffles, Dad pulled back and held her by the shoulders.

"Whatever possessed you to climb on the carousel?" he said. "Especially after I told you not to move. You could have been hurt!"

Why is he mad at me? thought Lucy. She didn't like the way grown-ups started out glad you were safe, then a few moments later, they got angry with you.

"I didn't mean it!" she said.

"If it wasn't for this lady," said Dad, finally looking up at Lucy's rescuer, "you could have been really hurt, love."

He stood up. "Thank you so much for helping my daughter. I'm very grateful to you. . . . Wait a minute—aren't you Tante Bep?"

"Arjo!" said Tante Bep. "I did not recognize you after all these years."

"Goodness," said Dad. "Well, welcome to Adelaide. We, ah, we couldn't find you."

"Instead," said Tante Bep, "I find you."

"Yes," laughed Dad. He leaned forward and kissed Tante Bep on both cheeks.

"This banana-clad child is our youngest, Calvin, and, of course, you've already met Lucy."

Tante Bep reached out to kiss Calvin. Calvin wiped off the kisses from each cheek as soon as she wasn't looking.

"Lucy doesn't normally ride baggage carousels," said Dad. "They're usually very well-behaved kids, as a rule."

"Really?" said Tante Bep. "I am thinking this is a naughty girl I have come all the way to Australia to visit."

Lucy thought this was most unfair. She had had a very hard day, what with Jacinta and the poem and Ms. Denny's letter and Paolo and almost being killed on a baggage carousel. Surely she deserved a little sympathy.

Dad put his arm around Lucy. "Yes, well, we all make mistakes."

"I hope I do not see more of this behavior," said

Tante Bep. "It makes me wonder what she is being taught at home." She looked straight at Dad and frowned. "Perhaps there is not enough discipline."

Dad opened his mouth, paused, then said, "Yes, well, let's just get your suitcase and go home. I think we could all do with a cool drink."

"Discipline," said Tante Bep. "That is what every child needs, Arjo. Discipline, and much of it."

Lucy and Calvin looked at each other. Lucy decided she didn't much like Tante Bep, even if she had saved her from certain death. How, she wondered, would they manage to share a bedroom for six weeks?

CHAPTER FOUR

"Lucy!" called Mum. "Time to get up."

Lucy squeezed her eyes shut and tried to make her dream come back.

Mum called through the door again, "Lucy, love, could you please collect the eggs for breakfast?"

Lucy opened one eye and noticed her great-aunt's empty bed. She had been so looking forward to showing Tante Bep her room, but last night, Tante Bep had not been interested at all. She didn't even say thank you when Lucy said she would sleep on the uncomfortable blow-up mattress and let Tante Bep have her bed. Lucy wondered where Tante Bep's manners were.

Not in the mood for a shower, Lucy pulled on some khaki shorts, then ferreted around in her drawer for a T-shirt. She had hidden the letter from Ms. Denny in that drawer. When her fingers accidentally touched it, she pulled her hand away. *Just don't think about it,* she said to herself, *and it will all go away.*

She walked out to the living room where Calvin was playing with his Legos. He had divided them up so that all the yellow bricks were in one neat pile and all the other colors were tossed together in a messy heap.

"Come on, Calvin," she said. "Let's go visit the chickens."

There were five eggs in the chicken coop in their backyard. Four of them were as warm as scones. One of them—the one she found hidden under some straw right at the back—was cold. Lucy placed it in her basket with the others.

Calvin leaned over the basket and gingerly touched one of the eggs. He shook his head. "Is touching the outside all right?" he asked, frowning.

"I think you're only allergic to the insides," said Lucy. "But better not touch them, just in case."

Calvin nodded. "My head puffed up."

"Yeah," said Lucy. "It was huge."

"Ginormous," said Calvin.

"Humungous!" said Lucy.

"Humungonormous!" said Calvin.

"Gigantosaurus!" said Lucy.

They cracked up laughing, then went quiet.

"It wasn't funny when it happened, though, was it?" said Lucy.

"I don't like hospitals," said Calvin.

Lucy smiled at her brother. "I know," she said.

And then, brightening up, she added, "Let's do an experiment. Let's test the eggs to see if they're rotten or not."

Calvin filled up a bucket, then Lucy gently put the eggs into the water.

"See, Calvin," said Lucy, "those ones have sunk, so that means they're good eggs and we can eat them. Well, I can eat them. You can't. But see this one? It's floating. Remember what Dad told us? If it floats—"

"It's a bad egg," finished Calvin.

Lucy took out the floating egg and cracked it on the back step. A terrible smell filled their noses.

"Um...maybe I shouldn't have done that," said Lucy, scraping the egg away with the side of her shoe. "Anyway, it's definitely a bad egg."

The van Loon family always ate bread, cheese, sliced meats, and boiled eggs for breakfast, just like people in Holland did. Lucy had never been to Holland, but both her parents had been born there.

"Pop the eggs in the egg cups, Lucy, love," said Dad, "while I get everything else ready."

Dad rubbed his bald patch while he thought about what to do next. Lucy thought his head looked a bit like a forest with a clearing in the middle.

Lucy went into the dining room with the egg basket. She put one egg in Mum's egg cup, one in Dad's, one in Tante Bep's, and one in her own.

Tante Bep and Calvin were already seated at the table. Lucy waited for Tante Bep to say what a helpful girl she was and how lucky her parents were to have her. Instead, Tante Bep picked up a cereal bowl and sipped straight from its rim. Lucy gasped.

"You're drinking from your bowl!"

"*Ja*," said Tante Bep. "Yes."

"Mum says we're not allowed to do that. We have to use a spoon for our soup or it's bad manners. That's right, isn't it, Calvin?"

Calvin nodded vigorously.

"But this is coffee," said Tante Bep. "In Europe, many people drink coffee from a bowl." She took another sip. "Mm, *lekker*. Delicious."

"I'm telling Mum," muttered Lucy. Even so, she secretly liked the idea of drinking from a bowl.

"And what about your manners, Lucy? I see you have not offered your ~~brother~~ an egg. Instead, you take the last one for yourself."

"Calvin can't have them," said Lucy. "Can you, Calvin?"

"We must not tell stories, Lucy," said Tante Bep.

"It's not a story," said Lucy. "Calvin *can't* have them. They make him sick."

Tante Bep shook her head in a disappointed way. "It is not nice to be greedy, Lucy."

Lucy gripped the tablecloth. Who did this lady think she was, accusing her like that? She didn't even know Lucy.

"I'm not greedy!" she said.

Calvin nodded. "She's not greedy."

Tante Bep raised an eyebrow and stared at Lucy. Lucy stared right back. She'd never been in a staring competition with an old person before. She was not about to lose.

"A good girl," said Tante Bep, "would give her egg to her little brother. If she were brought up properly."

Calvin's eyes switched from Lucy to Tante Bep and back again.

"Calvin can't eat eggs," said Lucy. "If he does, his head blows up and he could even die!"

Tante Bep laughed. It was an "I don't believe you" kind of laugh.

"I would too die," said Calvin. He put his hands around his throat and made choking sounds. He quite enjoyed doing this and carried on until he fell off his chair, where he writhed around on the floor. Lucy felt this was not helping.

"And now you encourage your brother to tell tales," said Tante Bep.

Lucy twisted the tablecloth so tightly that no ironing would ever get out the creases.

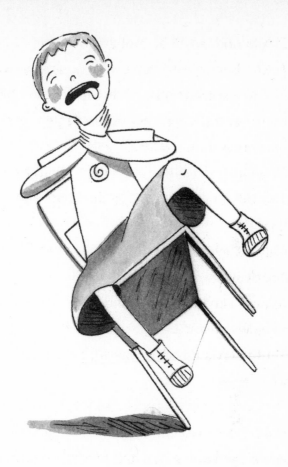

"I—am—not—greedy!" she shouted. "You take it back! You take it back!"

"Lucy!" said Dad, coming into the dining room. "What's all this about? Stop this yelling at once!"

"She said I was greedy and then she said the egg

and then Calvin and then she didn't believe me and then and then and then—"

There were too many words in Lucy's head. She couldn't make them into proper sentences, and anyway, Tante Bep was staring and Dad was staring and Calvin was rolling around on the floor and it was all too much. Lucy kicked her heels against her chair legs, opened her mouth, and shrieked.

Mum rushed into the room with her hair wrapped up in a towel. "Lucy!" she cried. "That's enough!"

Lucy took a deep breath, looked around at everyone's faces, and shrieked some more.

CHAPTER FIVE

"Lucy, what's got into you?" Dad had taken her into the kitchen for a talk. "You really embarrassed your mum and me with your carrying on."

"She started it," replied Lucy, pointing at Tante Bep through the French doors. "She shouldn't have called me names."

Dad sighed. "I know she can be a little… challenging, but you can't go around yelling at people. If you think you're going to lose your temper, you need to stop and think before it's too late. Perhaps you could practice counting to ten?"

"What for?" said Lucy. "I already know how to count."

"It would give you time to cool off before you say something you regret. It's what I do."

Lucy crossed her arms.

"Lucy," said Dad.

"I'll think about it," she replied.

Dad made Lucy go back into the dining room and say sorry to Tante Bep. Lucy wanted to know why no one made Tante Bep say sorry back. After all, she was the one who started it all.

"Apologize, Lucy," said Mum. "Immediately."

Lucy didn't want to get into any more trouble, so she made a decision. She would apologize out loud but take it back inside her head. She said, "I'm sorry, Tante Bep," but thought, *I'm not sorry at all.*

She said, "Please forgive me," but thought, *I will never forgive you. In fact, I unforgive you a million trillion times.*

"I accept your apology," said Tante Bep.

I unaccept your acceptance, thought Lucy.

When the phone rang, Lucy was relieved. It was Paolo asking if he could play with her. That led to Mum and Dad having an argument. Mum thought Lucy should be sent to her room to Think About

Her Behavior. Dad thought it would be better if Lucy was out of everyone's hair. Mum said it would be rewarding Lucy for being naughty. Dad said at least they'd have a bit of peace and quiet.

They sent Lucy out of the room while they debated it some more. She went and sat on the back doorstep, wishing Tante Bep would hurry up and go home. If it wasn't for her, she'd be allowed to play with Paolo.

Then Lucy spotted last year's phone book in the recycling bin. The new one had arrived that week and Dad had thrown out the old one. She picked it up and tore off a page. The *riiiiiiiiip* sound was very satisfying. She tore off another page and another. Before she knew it, she had ripped out twenty pages. She bunched each one up into a ball and threw them back in the recycling bin. For some strange reason, it made her feel calmer.

At last, Mum came outside. "Go on, then," she said. "Off you go to Paolo's. But please try to behave yourself."

Lucy suggested they play the dragon game.

"But just so you know," said Paolo, "I'm being a knight too."

"But, Paolo—"

"Being rescued is boring," said Paolo. "You just stand around waiting. Being a knight is heaps better. You get to fight dragons and have sword fights and stuff. And anyway, what if Blake and

Girang found out you were the knight and I was—"

"The princess?" said Lucy.

"No, not the princess," said Paolo. "We agreed, I was the prince."

Lucy pouted. "Someone has to be rescued."

"Either we're both knights or I won't play," said Paolo.

Lucy looked at him closely to see if he meant it. His arms were crossed, and he had a determined look on his face.

"Well, all right, then," she said. "Dogberry can be the princess."

Paolo looked horrified.

"But he's a boy dog!"

"So?" said Lucy.

"And a Rottweiler."

Lucy put her hands on her hips and gave him her fiercest look.

"I'll go get him," sighed Paolo.

When it was time to go home, Lucy said, "So do you promise to play with me at school on Monday?"

Paolo put his arms around Dogberry's neck and untied the princess cloak.

"Paolo?" said Lucy. "You said you'd play with me at school, but last week you just went off with Blake and Girang."

Paolo patted Dogberry on the head, not looking at her.

"Well?"

Paolo sighed deeply. "I promise."

"Good," said Lucy, and she climbed through the gap in their fence and into her own backyard.

As soon as Lucy walked into her bedroom, she knew something was wrong. For starters, all of her horse ornaments were gone. So were her glitter pens, her plaster cast of a chicken's footprint, and her special crystal echidna. Instead, there was a pile of Tante Bep's lotions and potions sitting on the dressing table.

Lucy looked around.

"Where are my things?" she asked Tante Bep. "They're normally right here." She pointed at the dresser.

"I put them in a box, out of the way," said Tante Bep.

Lucy saw the box beneath her dressing table. Nathan, her camel, was stuck inside it, stuffed cruelly upside down. Lucy would have to get him out later and 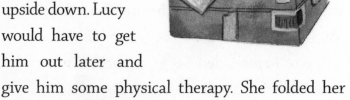 give him some physical therapy. She folded her arms crossly. She felt like making a big noise.

"Here, now," said Tante Bep, "you're not going to scream and shout again, are you? My old ears cannot take such loud sounds. Come, I want to show you something."

She guided Lucy over to the big suitcase that sat in the corner of the room. Tante Bep undid the latches and they snapped like brittle bones.

"Christmas is soon here," said Tante Bep, pulling an old sack out of the case. "But in only nine days—on the fifth of December—Sinterklaas will come to this house."

Another uninvited guest, thought Lucy.

"Sinterklaas is the Dutch Santa Claus," said Tante

Bep. "And he always brings his friend, Zwarte Piet. Black Piet."

Well, he can sleep on the sofa, thought Lucy. *My bedroom's crowded enough already.*

"Black Piet is black because he gets covered in soot when he slides down the chimney," said Tante Bep. "And all that dirt makes him in a very bad mood."

Tante Bep handed Lucy the sack. It was rough and smelled musty, like a locked-up room.

"If you have been good," she said, "Sinterklaas will give you a letter made of chocolate: *L* for Lucy, *ja*?"

Chocolate? Lucy smiled—just a little.

"But," said Tante Bep, suddenly frowning, "if you have been bad, Black Piet will put you in that coal sack and take you to Spain."

"To Spain!" said Lucy, dropping the sack. "He can't do that!"

"But he can," said Tante Bep. "Every year, he sends all the naughty children to Spain."

Lucy frowned. "Can I ever come back?"

"No," said Tante Bep. "You can never come back. This is why you must be clean and tidy and quiet while your *tante* is here."

Lucy narrowed her eyes. Now that she was in second grade, she didn't believe every crazy story she heard.

"You're making it up," she said, but her voice quavered.

"Am I?" said Tante Bep.

"And anyway," said Lucy, "Mum and Dad won't let him take me!"

"They won't know he's here," said Tante Bep. "They'll be fast asleep when he comes. And he is very, very quiet. This is why you must be a good girl. Understand?"

Lucy looked at the sack lying on the floor. It was a very big sack.

"Now," said Tante Bep. "Let me get back to cleaning this house. I did not know a house could get so dusty."

She hung the sack over Lucy's chair and left the room. Lucy stared at it. She was too young to go to Spain! She didn't even speak Spanish! She wanted to get rid of it, but the thought of touching it made her shudder. In the end, she used Tante Bep's hairbrush to lift it off the chair. Then she kicked it under the bed as far as it would go.

Lucy didn't sleep much that night. To take her mind off Black Piet, she made up a story in her head. It was about a clever young girl and a troll. The clever young girl was chained to the wall by her ankle with only a blow-up mattress to sleep on. The horrible old troll slept in what had once been the girl's own bed. This troll was a terrible snorer, and her breath was so hot that mice came out from their hiding places to toast marshmallows over her mouth. *One day*, thought the clever young girl, *one day I'll escape, and then everyone will know how mean the troll really is and she will be banished for ever and ever.*

CHAPTER SIX

Unfortunately for Lucy, the van Loon family never ate in front of the TV. That meant Lucy had to endure every meal sitting opposite Tante Bep. Each time she looked up, Lucy saw not an old Dutch woman but a troll with hot breath and nails so sharp they could carve a roast turkey.

Dinner on Sunday night was especially hard to tolerate because they were eating crusty bread, and Lucy hated crusts. Calvin was different. As long as his food was covered in tomato sauce, he would eat anything.

"Lucy," said her great-aunt, "pass me the cheese."

Please, thought Lucy. *Pass me the cheese, please.* She waited for Mum or Dad to correct Tante Bep. They said nothing.

"Honey," said Mum. "Tante Bep asked you for the cheese. Be a good girl and give it to her."

Lucy reached out and thrust it at her great-aunt.

Dad cut everyone a slice of crusty bread. *Yuk*, thought Lucy.

"This is Edam cheese, *ja*?" said Tante Bep. She dragged the slicer across it. A sliver of cheese came out through the slot like a sheet of paper.

"You're right, Tante Bep," said Dad. "It's Dutch Edam." He smiled broadly, smoothing nonexistent hair over his bald spot. "It was shipped here all the way from Holland, just for you," he added proudly.

"I prefer Gouda," said Tante Bep, laying the cheese on her bread. "But this will do, I suppose."

The smile on Dad's face sagged a little, like elastic that had gone slack.

Lucy ate some more of her bread. Now only the crusts were left. She slowly slipped them off the table and scrunched them up in her hand. Calvin saw her do this, and his eyes widened. She shook her head at him the tiniest little bit.

"I think I will wash the windows after we eat," said Tante Bep.

"Why?" said Dad.

"In Holland," said Tante Bep, "Dutch women clean their windows every week. That way, they don't get dirty." She looked at the dining room window and frowned.

Lucy felt underneath the tablecloth. She was looking for the little drawer under the tabletop. Where was it? Then she found it: a small knob, smooth, like a cold plum.

"I'm in charge of keeping the house clean," said Dad, "and the windows don't look dirty to me."

"You're in charge?" said Tante Bep, raising an eyebrow.

Lucy pulled out the drawer. *Quietly*, she thought, *quietly*. Calvin watched her closely, all the while munching on his bread-and-sauce sandwich.

"It's not right that a man be in charge of the home," said Tante Bep. "Hanneke, is this really true?"

"It's true," said Mum. "Arjo's the home manager."

Lucy slipped the crusts into the open drawer.

"He looks after the kids and does all the house-work, while I drive the City to Bay trolley," added Mum.

Tante Bep coughed on her cheese. "How strange," she said, picking up her bowl of coffee. "Well, that explains why the windows are dirty."

Dad opened his mouth to speak, but Mum frowned at him. He stuffed an egg into his mouth and chewed vigorously.

Lucy carefully shut the drawer, trying not to make any noise. If Tante Bep, or anyone else for that matter, found out what she was doing, she would be in big trouble.

CHAPTER
SEVEN

It was tiring being good for hours on end, and even more tiring worrying about Black Piet and that awful sack. Lucy had survived the weekend (sort of), but Tante Bep was staying five and a half more weeks! Lucy was almost glad to be back at school on Monday.

When the students sat down, there were two empty boxes on Ms. Denny's desk with a pile of papers between them. Only Lucy and Harriet had figured out the true meaning of these boxes.

One was for good drawings and one was for bad drawings, though they never knew which was

which till Ms. Denny had finished. Everyone else in the class just thought they were ordinary containers.

Ms. Denny lifted a sheet of paper off the pile. She held it first over the blue box, then over the red. Her earrings swung back and forth like dollhouse chandeliers. She dropped the paper into the blue box and picked up the next piece.

"Whose drawing do you think she's looking at now?" asked Lucy.

"If it's Jacinta's," said Harriet, "it'll go straight on the good pile."

"Mine won't," said Lucy. "It'll go straight on the bad pile. As usual."

Ms. Denny sucked on her peppermint. Lucy sucked in her breath. Harriet sucked on her braid.

When Ms. Denny had placed the last sheet of paper neatly in the blue box, she looked up. "I need two volunteers. Let's see...."

Jacinta's hand shot up.

"Lucy and Harriet," said Ms. Denny, "could you please come forward and help me put these up?"

Jacinta scowled. "She only asked you because she feels sorry for you," she whispered. "Poor old Lucy van Loony."

"It's not van Loony," hissed Lucy. "It's van Loon, and you know it rhymes with *bone*, not *moon*."

"What's that?" said Blake. "Lucy van Loony? Good one."

Paolo put his hand over his mouth to hide a laugh, but Lucy saw him. She stuck out her tongue at him.

"That's enough, Blake," said Ms. Denny. "Lucy, are you coming?"

Ms. Denny pushed the blue box toward them. "I'd like you girls to stick these up next to the blackboard, please."

"At the front," muttered Harriet. "That means the blue ones are the good ones."

"I'll take the red box to the back," continued Ms. Denny.

"The bad ones," whispered Lucy.

The class had been asked to draw a Christmas animal. As usual, Lucy had drawn her camel, Nathan. She reached into the box and tried to ignore Jacinta, who was mouthing "Lucy van Loony" while Ms. Denny was at the back of the classroom.

The first picture she pulled out was a donkey. The second picture, an ox. The third one . . .

"That's mine!" said Harriet happily. It was a sheep.

"Look at this one," said Lucy, turning up her nose. "It's a unicorn. Must be Jacinta's."

Harriet leaned over her shoulder. "Typical," she said. "And anyway, a unicorn's not an official Christmas animal."

Lucy quickly checked through the last drawings. A few cows, two donkeys, but no camel.

"Looks like mine'll be in the back again so no one can see it," said Lucy. "Well, I don't care. Ms. Denny can go jump."

She quickly wiped her eyes with the back of her hand. "Come on, let's put these up."

Harriet tore off great strips of sticky tape that shone like snail trails. Lucy preferred to use thumbtacks. She felt like pushing something sharp into the wall. When she picked up Jacinta's unicorn picture, she drove the tack straight through its eye and then felt much better. "My camel's much nicer than her unicorn," she said. "I wish I were a camel. They're really good spitters, so I could choose anyone in this room and spit on them from here. Right in their eye."

"Spitting's against the rules," said Harriet.

"Not if you're a camel," said Lucy.

"Good point," said Harriet. "So who would you pick?"

"Jacinta," said Lucy, "or Paolo, 'cause he wouldn't play with me at recess. I dunno. Maybe I would spit on Ms. Denny."

"You'd spit on whom?" said a voice from behind. And without turning around, Lucy knew exactly who it was.

CHAPTER EIGHT

Another turn in the Time Out chair was bad enough. Then it got worse: Ms. Denny asked Lucy about the letter.

"Did you give it to your parents?" she said. Her earrings swung back and forth, back and forth. "I hope they call me sometime this week. It's very important I talk to them."

When Lucy got home after school, she was on a mission. She ran into her bedroom and raced to her drawer. Making sure not to look at Black Piet's sack (which Tante Bep had rescued from underneath the bed), she pulled out Ms. Denny's letter and tucked it into her waistband. Then she ran out into the dining room. Dad was politely trying to wrestle a bottle of window cleaner out of Tante Bep's hands. They were too busy to notice Lucy as she slipped outside.

Her two favorite chickens, Apricot and Abigail, raced toward her, hoping for food. Lucy stepped over them and went into the chicken coop, where it was quiet and warm.

Taking out the letter, she turned it over in her hands, then took a deep breath. She tore it up once. She tore it up twice. She tore it up till it was nothing more than confetti. Then she kicked some straw over the top of it.

"There," she said. "No more letter."

It was different from when she had ripped up the phone book. Instead of feeling calmer, she felt squirmy, as if she had eaten too much pizza. *What if Black Piet finds out what I've done?* she wondered. She pushed that cold, scary thought away and went back inside.

Tante Bep was still in the dining room cleaning the windows. Dad had given up and was now in the laundry room, furiously mopping the floor. Lucy

got as far as the door to the dining room when
Tante Bep said, "Lucy, can we talk?"

Lucy jumped. Did Tante Bep know about the
letter?

Tante Bep tucked her rag into the pocket of her
apron. "Do you remember your promise to me to be
a good girl?"

Lucy remembered being told by Tante Bep to be a good girl. Technically, she did not remember any actual promising.

"Honesty is very important," said Tante Bep. "I would like to know my great-niece is an honest girl, *ja*? Is there something you would tell me?"

What does she know? thought Lucy. She was scared, but she was angry too. Angry that Tante Bep kept interfering in her life. She was very close to having a good shriek.

"Perhaps this will remind you," said Tante Bep. She went over to the dining room table and flung back the tablecloth. There was the secret drawer, opened, and filled to the brim with crusts.

Oh, thought Lucy. *That.*

The last thing Lucy wanted to do was touch stale crusts. Tante Bep made her clean out every last one. Some of them were moldy. They looked and felt like furry caterpillars. Tante Bep held out an empty ice-cream container for her to throw them in.

"You can feed them to the chickens," said Dad, standing in the doorway. "They won't mind a bit of mold." He wandered back into the laundry.

Why wasn't Dad stopping this woman? Why was he taking Tante Bep's side? Once again, Lucy felt like making a big noise. She felt like tipping all the chairs over and pulling the tablecloth off the table. She wanted to take that container and tip it over Tante Bep's head. She took another crust out of the drawer. Tante Bep's face was very close. Close enough to—

"Don't forget," said Tante Bep, lowering her voice, "Sinterklaas and Black Piet are coming in exactly one week."

Lucy went cold.

"You don't want him to take you in the middle of the night," whispered Tante Bep.

Lucy dropped the crust into the container and went out to feed the chickens.

When the chickens saw Lucy, they ran to her, jostling each other like feathery rugby players. Lucy scattered the crusts on the ground, then went into the chicken coop for a think.

This Black Piet business was a real worry.

Lucy knew she was a good girl. She was sure she was a good girl, even if she did get into trouble sometimes. Yes, it was everyone else who was wrong.

But then a horrible thought dropped into her

head like a huge stone thrown in a bucket. What if Lucy van Loon was really a bad person and she just didn't know it? She pushed the thought away as hard as she could, but it kept coming back, harder and harder, louder and louder. Could she be a bad girl? Could she be Lucy the Bad?

Lucy realized she would have to find out as soon as possible. Black Piet was coming in exactly one week's time. If people thought she was bad, well, she would show them different. She could be good Lucy. She *would* be good Lucy. That'd show them. From now on, she would be a new person with a new name, and that name was Lucy the Good.

CHAPTER NINE

Lucy spent the rest of the school week practicing being Lucy the Good. Sometimes, she forgot and did things like stick out her tongue at Jacinta. Then Black Piet would pop into her mind and she would quickly pretend she was just licking her lips. Another time, she was about to give Paolo a pinch on his leg for ignoring her, when she saw—or thought she saw—Black Piet hanging around by the monkey bars with a sack over his shoulder.

Harriet told her she was just imagining things, but one lunch break, she was sure she saw Black

Piet standing in the doorway of the girls' bath-room.

The next time she looked, she just saw shadows. With less than a week till Sinterklaas Day, Lucy had to figure out this good and bad business before it was too late.

"You have to help me," said Lucy.

It was Friday lunchtime, and Lucy and Harriet were down by the library. Harriet was practicing handstands, and Lucy was drinking out of a plastic cereal bowl she had brought from home. This attracted the attention of some kids walking past.

"It's how they do it in Europe," she called out.

"What sort of help do you need?" asked Harriet, speaking in her upside-down voice.

"I have to know if I'm bad or not. Otherwise, Black Piet will get me," said Lucy. "My turn."

Lucy took a run-up and charged at the wall. She planted her hands on the ground and flung her

legs up in the air. *Slap slap*. The backs of her heels struck the wall and her arms locked. A perfect handstand.

"But I told you already," said Harriet. "Black Piet

isn't real. That Bep lady just made him up to scare you. And anyway, you're not bad."

"Tante Bep thinks I am, since I got mad at her. What if she's right?"

"She's not," said Harriet. "She just hates big noises."

Blood was pressing against the backs of Lucy's eyes, making it hard to think. She kicked off the wall and stood up. "Let's make a list of what makes some things good and some things bad."

The two girls sat cross-legged on the ground.

"We should do it properly," said Harriet. "You know. Officially."

She got out a sheet of paper and two colored pencils. She wrote *GOOD* on one side of the page in blue pencil and *BAD* on the other side in red. Lucy picked up her bowl and took another sip.

"What about the good scissors?" said Lucy.

In her house, only grown-ups were allowed to touch those.

Harriet wrote *good scissors* carefully on the GOOD page.

"What else?"

Harriet put her braid in her mouth so she could think better.

"I know," said Lucy. "Write down *good china, good teapot,* and *good pencils.*"

Then she remembered all those times she'd been in the garden after it had rained. When she came back inside, Dad always told her to take off her shoes to protect his good clean floor.

Soon, their list was so long they needed another sheet of paper. Some of the things on the blue page were:

good scissors
good china
good teapot
good pencils
good clean floor
good manners
goody-two-shoes
goodness me!

On the red page, they had:

bad books
bad news
bad temper
bad behavior
bad habits
bad luck
bad breath
gone bad

"Dirt," said Harriet, polishing her left shoe with spit, "is also bad. That's what Mum says, anyway."

Lucy looked down at her hands. They were covered with little specks of gravel from all the handstands she'd done. Her nails were black too. Dark little crescents that would take a fair bit of scrubbing to clean.

"I don't think these lists are really getting us anywhere," said Harriet.

Lucy looked down at the pages in her hands, willing them to give her an answer.

"Wait a second," she said. "You know what we've left off?"

"What?"

Lucy smiled slowly. "Eggs," she replied. "Good eggs and bad eggs."

"What's so special about eggs?" said Harriet.

Lucy folded up the lists and put them in her pocket.

"I have an idea," she said. "But first, I need to find Paolo."

CHAPTER TEN

"Got it," said Paolo, climbing through the gap in the fence between their two houses. He was carrying a garbage bag that he handed to Lucy. It was Saturday, the day after Lucy had had her Big Idea.

"Great," said Lucy, peering in the bag. "This is just what I need."

"What do you want it for anyway?" said Paolo.

Lucy walked over to the cast-iron bathtub in the yard. It had legs shaped like lions' feet. Lucy liked to think the tub had wandered into their backyard one day and decided to stay. Normally the bathtub was empty. Today Lucy had filled it up with water.

"Dad showed me how good eggs sink and bad eggs float," she said. "I think other things must too."

"Are you sure?" said Paolo. "It sounds stupid."

"Don't stay, then," said Lucy. "I'll just tell everyone your sisters put makeup on you and tie up your hair in bows."

"No, it's okay," he said quickly. "I'll stay."

"Good," said Lucy. "We'll do one of my things first."

"Why not one of mine?"

"Because it's my house and I'm the boss," said Lucy.

Potatoes seemed a good place to start. Lucy bent down and threw one in the tub. It sank, so it must be good. The apples floated, so they must be bad.

"Try the Weetabix," said Paolo.

Lucy threw it in. The biscuit floated to begin with, then slowly sank to the bottom.

"I wonder what that means," said Paolo.

Next, Lucy threw in a lightbulb, some Dutch salted licorice, and a string of wooden beads. She dropped in Countess Esmeralda (her least-favorite doll), a paper clip, an almost empty box of tissues, and a stapler. Surely, she was getting closer to the answer.

Paolo opened up his bag and threw in a bicycle pump, a saw, and an old plastic jack-in-the-box.

"What else?" said Lucy.

She looked around until she spotted a chicken feather on the ground. Then she saw Apricot giving herself a dust bath over by the chicken coop.

"I know," she said, smiling.

Apricot wasn't as keen to go in the bathtub as Lucy had hoped. She flapped her wings and pecked and clucked.

"Come on, Paolo. Help me," said Lucy.

"I'm not sure this is such a good idea," said Paolo, stepping back.

"Paolo!"

Apricot wriggled out of her hands and ran behind the shed. Lucy followed her, wondering if she had the power to talk to animals. She closed her eyes and concentrated. *Stay still, Apricot,* she thought. *Stay still and let me put you in the tub.* She made a dive for her, grabbed her feathery body, and raced back to the tub.

"Quick!" she cried. "Move out of the way."

Paolo jumped aside, and Lucy dipped Apricot's feet in the water. Apricot squawked, flapped, and

escaped once more with an angry *bok bok bok!* Lucy sighed.

"I s'pose we've tested enough things," she said sadly.

"So what's the answer to the experiment?" said Paolo.

Lucy frowned. "I still don't know," she said. "I just have to keep thinking."

"Lucy! Lucy! I need you." It was Tante Bep.

Paolo looked in the direction of the house, then at the bathtub, then at Lucy. He took off through the gap in the fence.

"Coming, Tante Bep," said Lucy tiredly. She hoped her great-aunt hadn't discovered yet another thing Lucy had done wrong.

CHAPTER ELEVEN

"This afternoon," said Tante Bep, passing Lucy a glass of apple juice, "you and I will bake Dutch cookies for Sinterklaas Day."

Tante Bep, Dad, Calvin, and Lucy were in the kitchen. Calvin was picking the raisins out of a piece of raisin toast. He handed them to Lucy, who squished them into one big raisin, which she popped into her mouth.

"What are we going to bake?" said Lucy cautiously.

She still hadn't forgiven Tante Bep for making her clean out her crusts.

"*Speculaas*," said Tante Bep.

"Yum," said Dad. "I buy those for us from the market, don't I, Lucy?"

Lucy nodded.

"Bought *speculaas*?" said Tante Bep. "Don't you make them yourself, Arjo?"

Dad rubbed the top of his head. "I'm very busy," he said. "I don't have time to go baking cookies every day of the week."

"No time?" said Tante Bep. "But you don't have a job."

Dad's eyes looked like they were about to pop out of his head and roll around on the kitchen counter.

"I'm the home manager," he spluttered. "That's my job. It doesn't leave a lot of free time, you know."

"So it seems," said Tante Bep. "Since you don't have time to bake *speculaas*."

Dad got up and cleared the table. Lucy saw his lips moving. "One," he seemed to be saying, "two, three…"

A little later, Tante Bep suggested that the fridge needed cleaning and Dad abruptly excused himself, taking Calvin with him.

Lucy stayed. She loved cooking. She loved the mixing, she loved the baking smell, she loved the mess, but most of all, she loved licking the bowl.

Tante Bep got out a package of flour, some sugar, some spices, a stick of butter, and a carton of milk. Then she sat down on a stool and folded her hands.

"What are you going to do next?" said Lucy.

"*You* are going to take two cups of flour and put it in that bowl," she said.

"You want me to do it?" said Lucy.

"Of course," said Tante Bep. "How else will you learn?"

Lucy smiled. Mostly when grown-ups said you could help with the cooking, they meant Pretend Helping. They let you stir the bowl once or twice, or maybe crack an egg. Tante Bep was letting Lucy make the *speculaas* all by herself. It made her feel grown-up.

Lucy put all the ingredients in to the bowl and stirred them in big, stiff circles. Then she lifted out the big blob of dough and dropped it on the counter. She imagined she was Miss Lucy, the

famous baker. People couldn't stop talking about the seven-year-old who made cookies so delicious, people would pay one hundred dollars for a single bite.

"You must now knead the dough," said Tante Bep, "like so." She made pounding motions with her fists. "I like to do this when something make me angry."

"Why?" asked Lucy.

"It always make me feel better. You try."

Lucy thumped the dough with her knuckles, pushing it back and forth. She found kneading very satisfying.

"Now roll it out like so," said Tante Bep.

Lucy picked up the rolling pin. It was made of marble and was very heavy. *People will come from all around the country just to watch Miss Lucy bake,* she thought.

"*Ja,* that's right," said Tante Bep. "Now roll the other way."

Lucy imagined the prime minister—no! the queen, no! a TV producer—wanted to meet her. "We'd like to offer you your own cooking show, Miss Lucy," said the TV producer. "We'll pay you one million dollars."

Tante Bep lifted a wooden windmill off the wall. "Do you know what this is?" she said. "We're going to press the dough into this."

"But that's a decoration," said Lucy. "We'll get into trouble."

Tante Bep laughed. She sounded almost friendly. "It's also for making cookies," she said. "It's a mold."

Tante Bep showed Lucy how to press the dough into the mold, then cut off the edges. Soon, there were rows of windmill-shaped cookies sitting on a tray waiting to be baked. Lucy handed the tray carefully to Tante Bep. Tante Bep opened the oven door and slid them inside.

"I remember the time Johanna bake *speculaas*,"

said Tante Bep, sitting back down on her stool. "She bake them for Sinterklaas Day."

"Who's Johanna?" said Lucy.

"My little sister," said Tante Bep. "She live in Denmark now. But back then, when we were childrens, we all live in a small house in Maasland in Holland. It was the war, and there was not much food. *Nee*," she added. "No. Not much food. There were times when all my mother can cook are tulip bulbs. Can you imagine?"

Tulip bulbs? Lucy thought of the onion-shaped bulbs Mum planted in the garden every year. They were covered in dirt and didn't look very tasty.

"How did she cook them?" Lucy asked.

"She slice them up and make soup. Ugh. *Niet lekker*. Not a good taste. And not very good for your insides."

Lucy thought of her crusts and how she didn't like them. That seemed like nothing compared to eating tulip bulbs every day.

"During the war, sometimes it is very hard to get sugar or butter or spices. One day, a friend come to the back door with a bag of these things. It is Sinterklaas Eve. Johanna take these things and bake them into little windmill cookies, like you have. Oh, the smell is wonderful. *Prachtig.* For tea that night, we ate *speculaas.* Only *speculaas.* It was the best meal I ever eat." Tante Bep closed her eyes and smiled to herself.

Lucy wasn't sure what to say. She felt as if Tante Bep had given her a special gift by telling her this story.

"When I see you make the *speculaas,*" said Tante Bep, opening her eyes, "*ja,* that give me a happy memory."

Lucy smiled. She wondered if Tante Bep might actually like her.

CHAPTER TWELVE

Lucy had such a lovely weekend with Tante Bep, she completely forgot about Black Piet. Almost. About five minutes after school started on Monday, she received a very clear reminder.

"Lucy," said Ms. Denny, "I still haven't heard from your parents. Are you sure you gave them my letter?"

Lucy felt squirmy inside. Lucy the Good wouldn't lie, especially since it was Sinterklaas Eve. Sinterklaas and Black Piet were coming that very night. They would stand over her bed and decide if she was good or bad. If she told Ms. Denny how she had ripped up the letter...

"Um," said Lucy.

"Blake!" said Ms. Denny. "Put that down! Faces and glue do not mix.... No, Blake, I'm sure Kate does not want her face stuck to the furniture.... Blake!"

Ms. Denny walked to the back of the classroom.

That was close, thought Lucy.

After lunch was show-and-tell. Two people were chosen each week to bring something special from home. Lucy had brought along Nathan, nicely dressed up in a new scarf Tante Bep had knitted for him the day before. The scarf was made of bright orange wool—Holland's color.

Lucy hoped she'd get to go first, especially since Jacinta was the other person on the roster. *Perhaps I've got the power to control people's minds,* she thought. *Pick me, Ms. Denny. Pick Lucy van Loon. Lucy van Loon. Lucy van Loon. Lucy van—*

"Jacinta," said Ms. Denny, "up you come."

Lucy scowled.

When Jacinta got to the front, she held up her show-and-tell item.

"Another unicorn?" said Ms. Denny.

This one was bigger, fluffier, and cuter than any other unicorn Jacinta had brought in before. It had bright white fur, a gleaming silver horn, and a multicolored mane. Lucy thought of scruffy old Nathan sitting in her bag.

"And what's her name?" said Ms. Denny.

"Fluffy Rainbow," replied Jacinta.

Fluffy Rainbow! Lucy and Harriet rolled their eyes. The boys in the back sniggered.

"She's very pretty," said Ms. Denny.

"People can pet her if they want."

Jacinta walked down each aisle, letting the other students stroke her toy. Lucy stared at the unicorn's fur. How soft it must feel. How nice and velvety.

When it was Lucy's turn to pat her, Jacinta cried, "Wait!" and pulled Fluffy Rainbow away. "Your hands are dirty. Ms. Denny, Lucy's hands are all dirty."

"No, they're not!" said Lucy.

"Let me see," said Ms. Denny, stepping out from behind her desk.

Lucy held out her hands, fully expecting them to be clean. Instead, she saw two black palms looking back at her.

"How did that get there?" Lucy said.

"Handstands," whispered Harriet.

"I think you'd better go scrub those clean," said Ms. Denny.

"Now?" said Lucy.

"Now," said Ms. Denny. "Or you'll make your workbook all dirty. Run along to the bathroom."

Lucy didn't move.

"Off you go," said Ms. Denny.

Lucy still didn't move.

"What's the matter, Lucy?"

"She doesn't go in school bathrooms," explained Harriet. "She holds it till she gets home."

Some of the students giggled. Ms. Denny sighed a grown-up sigh. "Lucy," she said, "please."

"You better go," whispered Harriet. "Remember: you're Lucy the Good, and Lucy the Good obeys the rules."

Lucy thought hard. A good girl would wash her hands. That was true. A good girl would go to the bathroom. *But I don't want to! Why should I?*

"Only babies are scared of the bathroom," said Jacinta, as quietly as possible.

Lucy shot her a look. Jacinta made sure Ms. Denny couldn't see her, then she put her thumb in her mouth and sucked it like a baby.

"Come on, Lucy," said Ms. Denny. "Off you go. I promise, it's perfectly safe."

Lucy couldn't move. Her cheeks got hotter and hotter. She turned around and noticed her camel picture all the way in the back. It reminded her of all the mean things Ms. Denny had done to her. Never putting her pictures in the good pile. Always sending her to the Time Out chair. That familiar rumble of anger began to stir inside her.

"Lucy," said Ms. Denny, "we haven't got all day."

Lucy clenched and unclenched her hands.

"What a baby," whispered Jacinta. She sucked on her thumb again, holding her unicorn close to her chest, as if it might get germs if Lucy touched it. "Wah, wah, wah."

"Lucy!" said Ms. Denny.

Other kids in the class started sucking their thumbs too.

"Lucy's a baby."

"Lucy's scared of the bathroom."

"What a loony."

"That's enough, class. If you don't settle down,

you'll be staying in during lunch time," said Ms. Denny. "Lucy. Bathroom. Now!"

At that moment, Lucy knew only one thing. There was no way she, Lucy van Loon, was going to the bathroom.

The anger inside her made its way up to her throat. It was now too late to count to ten, and she didn't have any *speculaas* dough to pound. What's more, she no longer cared about being Lucy the Good. Lucy the Good was gone. Lucy the Good was over.

Now there was only Lucy the Bad-tempered. Lucy the Badly Behaved. Lucy the Bad Apple. In short, there was only Lucy the Bad. The anger didn't stop in her throat but kept going, up past her teeth and out of her mouth.

"Eeeeeeeahhhhhhhh!" she shrieked. "I won't go! I won't go!"

Then everyone fell silent.

But not in a good way.

CHAPTER THIRTEEN

Lucy was in big trouble now. It was Spain in a coal sack for sure. And what was worse, Ms. Denny was going to call her parents. She'd said so, shortly after Lucy had screamed the place down.

Lucy had to get home. She had to stop Ms. Denny from talking to Dad. Unfortunately, Harriet's mum was giving her a lift, and she had to stop at the newsstand for the paper. *Come on,* thought Lucy. *Hurry up, hurry up, hurry up!*

When Mrs. Spiegel finally pulled into Berry Street, Lucy ripped off her seat belt and jumped out of the car. "Thanks for the lift!" she called as she bolted down the driveway.

Lucy ran into the house and straight to the phone. She took hold of the handset and lifted it up. She could hear the dial tone droning: *brrrrrrrrrrrr*. She made sure no one was nearby, then laid the handset down on the telephone table and put a book over the top of it. There was no way Ms. Denny could get through now.

The fear was gone, but all the same, Lucy's head was filled with hot, red thoughts. She went outside, snuck past Dad, who was weeding in the back garden, and slipped into the chicken coop. She shut the door behind her, sat down on an upturned bucket, and had a good think.

All she knew was, she'd tried so hard to be Lucy the Good, and it hadn't gotten her anywhere. Everything she did turned out wrong. Her teacher hated her. Her schoolmates teased her. She'd thought Tante Bep was starting to like her, but Black Piet was coming tonight, and Tante Bep had left out a sack for him!

Then there were her parents. Dad had taken Tante Bep's side when Tante Bep found her crusts. Mum was never around. It seemed like nobody was on her side. Lucy wondered, did they even like her? And a worse thought, did they even love her? Tears fell from her eyes, leaving silver squiggles down her cheeks. She tried to cry quietly so Dad wouldn't

hear. *Nobody cares about me*, she thought. *No one at all.*

Then she heard Dad making splashing noises in the outdoor bathtub.

"What's this?" she heard him say. "What on earth's a jack-in-the-box doing in the bathtub? And isn't that my stapler?"

Uh-oh, thought Lucy. She jumped up and ran out of the shed before Dad could say anything. There was something she had to do, and she had to do it right away.

CHAPTER FOURTEEN

"Where do you want me to go?" said Harriet. She was standing in the doorway of her apartment wearing a too-large apron. "I'm s'posed to help cook supper."

"We're going to the creek," said Lucy. "Quick. We have to go now."

"We're not allowed to go to the creek by ourselves," said Harriet. "It's against the rules."

"But this is an emergency," said Lucy.

"I can't," said Harriet, looking over her shoulder. "I'll get in trouble."

"Fine!" said Lucy. "I'll go by myself!"

She charged down the street past Paolo's place.

He was sitting on the porch, making his toy cars do stunts off the top step. Lucy turned her head away and walked quickly by.

"Hey!" called Paolo. "Where are you going?"

Lucy kept walking.

"I said, where are you going?"

She didn't even turn around.

At the end of Berry Street, Lucy turned the corner into Bottle Crescent. At the end of the crescent was a park, and beyond the park, a creek. Lucy walked through the park and under the swings. When she got to the fence, she climbed over it and half walked, half slid down the embankment.

When she got to the bottom, she realized Paolo had followed her.

"Come on, Lucy," he called. "Aren't you talking to me?"

Lucy sat down on a rock and took off her shoes and socks.

"What are you doing?" he said.

"You never talk to me at school," said Lucy, "except to be mean to me, so why should I talk to you now?"

"But I want to know," said Paolo. "C'mon, tell me what you're doing."

"You're my enemy now," said Lucy, "but if you must know, I'm doing an experiment. I'm going to find out if I'm good or bad."

"Another experiment?" said Paolo. "What kind?"

"Same as the egg one," said Lucy. She stuffed her socks into her shoes and stood up.

"The bathtub thing?"

"Yes," she said. "Good things sink and bad things float, so I'm going to go in the water and see which one I am."

Paolo looked at the creek. It crept along through a maze of rocks, rubbish, and fallen tree branches.

"It's not very deep," he said.

Lucy took off her watch. "It's deep enough," she said.

"It'll be cold," he added.

"Tough."

Lucy waded out into the creek. Paolo was right. It wasn't very deep. The water only came halfway up her shins. She waded out a bit farther to see if it was deeper in the middle.

"I'm not diving in to save you," said Paolo. "I've got my new boots on."

Lucy ignored him. The water was only up to her knees, but she figured she could still float in it. Float or sink. She waded forward, feeling the rocks with her toes.

"This is dumb," said Paolo. "I'm going home."

"No one invited you anyway," said Lucy.

She didn't look at him, but she heard him tramping back up the embankment.

Lucy stepped onto a rock, which wobbled beneath her foot. She tried to get her balance back by waving her arms in the air like a bird.

She steadied herself and stepped out once again onto a different rock. This was wobbly too, and slippery. Her foot slid off to the side. She tried to grab

the air for support. It didn't work. She fell into the water with a splash.

Lucy had fallen on her bottom and was now wet up to her waist. Coughing and spluttering, she slapped the water with her hands.

"I hate everything!" she cried.

When she'd finished coughing, Lucy braced her hands on a fallen log and tried to stand up. She couldn't. Her foot was jammed between two rocks. She yanked her leg, but it was no use. She was stuck. She hit the water again. If only she could detach her leg the way blue-tongue lizards could lose their tails! Then she could escape and her leg would grow back in a few weeks' time.

"Leg," she commanded, "I order you to drop off!"

She closed her eyes and willed it to obey her. When she opened her eyes, it was still attached.

I am *bad*, thought Lucy. Dad had made her promise to never ever go down to the creek without an adult. No matter what. And what had she done? She'd gone and done it anyway! Why couldn't she be a good girl for once? It seemed everyone was right about her. She was bad all the way through.

"Help," whispered Lucy, then a little more loudly, "Paolo! Help! I'm stuck!"

But she knew Paolo must be halfway home by now. There was no way he could hear her. A sob expanded in her throat, inflating like a marshmallow in a microwave. She imagined herself stuck there all night. What if it rained? There could be a flash flood and the water would come up higher and higher. She would drown before anyone came to save her. She'd never see Mum and Dad again. She'd never see Calvin. Even the thought of never seeing Tante Bep again brought a tear to her eye.

"This is the worst day of my life!" she howled. "I don't want to die!"

CHAPTER FIFTEEN

If only she had the power to send thought waves to Dad! *Come and rescue me,* thought Lucy. *I'm down by the creek. Hurry, Dad, hurry, before the creek floods and I die.* She closed her eyes and wished with all her might.

"Lucy?" said Dad. "Lucy!"

Lucy opened her eyes. Had she imagined it? Had she really summoned Dad with her exceptional mental powers? She looked up and saw him standing high on the bank of the creek, looking worried.

"A little birdie told me you might be here."

It worked, thought Lucy. *I'm saved!*

"Stay where you are, honey. I'm coming in."

"My foot's stuck," she cried.

Dad scrambled down the embankment and waded straight into the creek. He didn't care about getting his boots wet. He reached into the water and pulled the rocks apart. Lucy's foot was free again.

But now that she was safe, thinking of her

near-death experience made her burst into tears. She could hardly see a thing for crying. She did, however, feel Dad's arms around her as he lifted her out of the creek. She wasn't going to die.

Back at home, Mum fetched a large towel and wrapped it around her daughter. Lucy told her parents about her experiment. "I just needed to know if I was a good person or not," she finished.

"You poor love," said Mum. "Still, you shouldn't have gone to the creek. You could have drowned! And then what would we have done?"

"I didn't really think about it prop'ly," said Lucy.

Mum kissed her on the forehead.

Calvin handed her his favorite yellow truck. "How long were you stuck in the creek?" he asked.

"Ages," said Lucy. "It was really uncomfortable too. The creek bed had lots of stones in it."

Lucy paused. If she was sitting on the creek bed, that meant she'd sunk, not floated. In all the excitement, she'd forgotten about the experiment!

"I'm a good person!" she cried in surprise.

"Of course, you are," said Mum. "Did you really believe you weren't?"

Lucy thought about it some more. Sure, she screamed sometimes, but she did other things too. She always made sure Calvin stayed away from food that might make him sick. She let Tante Bep have her bed (even if Tante Bep didn't appreciate it). She looked after the chickens, and she always tried hard at school, especially with her drawings and poems. It was a pretty impressive list of good things, now that she thought about it. Lucy may have sat in cold water all afternoon, but she began to feel warm inside.

"Eggs and humans are very different things, love," said Dad. "Floating or sinking doesn't work that way for us. And anyway, I don't need any experiment to tell me what you are. You've got a good heart, and that's the most important thing."

Dad gave her shoulder a squeeze, then turned and glared at Tante Bep.

"Lucy," said Tante Bep, holding her hand across her mouth. "Oh, Lucy."

She got up and left the room.

"Your great-aunt's very shaken up," said Mum. "We all are. Tante Bep didn't realize you'd take that Black Piet story so seriously. She was wrong to scare you like that."

"If I'd known she was telling you such tales," said Dad, "I would've—"

Mum shook her head.

"What?" said Calvin. "What would you have done, Dad?"

"Let's just say she was very naughty, and she shouldn't have done it," he finished.

Lucy was amazed at the idea that an adult could be naughty. She wondered if Mum and Dad would tell Tante Bep off. She liked the sound of that.

Lucy spent the next hour telling her parents everything. She told them about her problems at school. She told them how she'd tried to be good but couldn't seem to get it right. She told them about Jacinta and Ms. Denny and her camel pictures and

show-and-tell and seeing Black Piet everywhere.
Mum and Dad didn't say much. They just listened.

"You know what?" said Lucy. "When I scream and
scream, it all gets worse."

Mum and Dad looked at each other and smiled in
a relieved sort of way.

"I'm just thinking, is there some way you could
get your anger out in a quieter way?" asked Mum.
"Something that would help you feel calmer."

Lucy paused for a moment. "The other day, I ripped up the old phone book, and that made me feel better."

"Ah ha," said Dad, rubbing his hands together. "What say I scout around, gather up a few phone books from around the neighborhood? You could rip them up to your heart's content."

Lucy smiled. It was worth a shot.

Tante Bep didn't join them for supper. She stayed in Lucy's room with the door shut. When it was time to go to bed, Lucy tapped on the door softly. She felt funny about sharing a room with Tante Bep tonight.

"Come," said Tante Bep.

Lucy pushed open the door with one finger. Tante Bep was sitting on the bed with the coal sack draped across her lap. Lucy took a step back.

"Wait," said Tante Bep. "Please, I want to show you something." She picked up a pair of scissors lying on her lap. Mum's good scissors. *Snip snip*

snip. She cut the coal sack in two. Then she took those pieces and cut them in two as well. *Snip snip snip.* She cut up the rest of the sack. Neither of them spoke until the floor was covered with scraps of material. Enough to make a patchwork quilt.

"Please come here, Lucy." Tante Bep patted the bed beside her.

Lucy took a big step over the sack scraps and sat down.

"You and I," said Tante Bep, "we have not been the best of friends, have we?"

Lucy shrugged her shoulders.

"It's okay," said Tante Bep. "It is my fault. I shouldn't have tried to scare you like that. It was very wrong of me."

Lucy said nothing. Secretly, she was enjoying a

grown-up saying sorry to her, rather than the other way around. She wanted it to last a bit longer.

"To think I could have lost my great-niece today." Tante Bep shut her eyes and shuddered. "*Nee*. I could not bear that."

"Don't worry," said Lucy. "Dad saved me."

"There is more," said Tante Bep. "Your mother told me about your brother. She say he has allergy to eggs. She say everything you say to me is true."

"It is true," said Lucy.

"Please let me apologize for saying you are greedy. You are not a greedy girl, Lucy. *Nee*, you are not. You are very generous. You let me share your room and your bed, and I don't even say thank you. Let me say it now. *Dank je wel*. Thank you."

Once more, Lucy felt warm inside.

"I'd like us to be friends," said Tante Bep. "What do you say about that?"

Lucy thought for a moment. A long moment. She didn't want to forgive Tante Bep too easily. "Maybe we could bake some more *speculaas*," she said at last.

"*Ja*, I'd like that," said Tante Bep. "I could teach you some other Dutch recipes also, *ja*?"

Lucy nodded.

"*Goed so*," said Tante Bep. "Good." She reached over and patted Lucy on the hand. Lucy noticed Tante Bep didn't assume she would get a hug. *Maybe in a couple of weeks*, thought Lucy. *I might let her hug me then.*

"Now," said Tante Bep. "Let us set out the clogs by the fireplace. Sinterklaas comes tonight, and he need somewhere to put the chocolate letters. But don't worry," she added, "he will not bring Black Piet."

CHAPTER SIXTEEN

"I should've been there," said Harriet. "You could have died!"

"I know," said Lucy, smiling. The thought of *almost* dying was really quite exciting. "I prob'ly would've if it wasn't for Dad."

"And me," said Paolo, coming over to the classroom steps to join them. "I was the one who told your dad where you were."

Lucy smiled to herself. She knew the truth: Dad had come because of her mental powers.

"Did someone almost die?" said Jacinta.

She climbed the steps and sat down too. So did Kate and Amal and Priya.

"Lucy did," said Harriet.

"Yeah," said Paolo. "She almost drowned, 'cept I went and got help."

"My foot got trapped in the river," said Lucy, "and the water was rising and rising. It was almost up to my neck and I was about to go under. But Dad turned up just in time and rescued me."

She paused to sip from her bowl of milk, sneaking a look at Jacinta to see how she was taking it. Jacinta was staring at Lucy with eyes as big as hockey pucks.

"I wish I'd almost died and been rescued just in time," said Kate wistfully.

Some other kids came over and joined them—Blake and Girang and Tran. Lucy noticed the trend for drinking milk the Dutch way had caught on. Several of the kids had brought bowls from home and were sipping chocolate milk out of them.

"I got a present from the Dutch Santa Claus too," said Lucy. "It's Sinterklaas Day today."

She reached into her bag and took out a large chocolate letter *L* with a bite taken out of it.

"I wish I was Dutch," said Kate.

Jacinta looked longingly at the chocolate.

As Lucy nibbled a bit off, Ms. Denny appeared in the doorway of their classroom. Miniature red and green parrot earrings hung from her ears, each parrot swinging on its own perch.

"Lucy," said Ms. Denny. "Could I have a word with you before class?"

Lucy looked at Harriet and grimaced. *Here we go,* she thought. *I'm in so much trouble for everything I've done.*

Ms. Denny showed Lucy into the classroom and shut the door.

"I've just been speaking to your dad on the phone," she said. "I tried to ring him yesterday for a chat, but he said the phone had been off the hook all night for some reason."

"Oh?" said Lucy.

"He explained quite a few things to me, actually, about why you've been getting so angry."

"The last time I threw a tantrum, you were trying to make me go to the bathroom, and everyone was picking on me, and Jacinta wouldn't let me touch her unicorn," Lucy blurted out.

Ms. Denny was quiet for a moment. "I'm sorry, Lucy," she said. "I didn't fully realize what was going on, and I was flustered. Let's just say I didn't handle the situation at all well, and you bore the brunt of it. How about this: I promise to listen to you if you promise that any time you're about to yell, you come and talk to me first."

"It's usually too late then," sighed Lucy. "The yell is already on its way."

"Where does the yell begin?"

Lucy pointed to her tummy. "In here," she said. "Then it goes up here." She pointed at her chest. "And here." She touched her throat. "And comes out here." She opened her mouth.

"I wonder," suggested Ms. Denny, "what if you let me know when it's in your tummy?"

"Before it starts going up, you mean?"

Ms. Denny nodded. "We might be able to stop it then."

Lucy had never thought of that before. It was worth a try. "Okay," she said.

"There's one other thing," said Ms. Denny. "Your

father said you think I don't like your pictures. What makes you believe that?"

"You always hang them up in the back where no one can see them."

"Oh, Lucy." Ms. Denny looked at her kindly. Her parrot earrings swung back and forth, and Lucy wondered if they might start squawking. "Here," she said. "Come and sit in my chair behind the teacher's desk. I want to show you something."

Lucy went over and sat down slowly. It felt strange being in the teacher's seat. But good strange.

"I spend a lot of time sitting or standing behind this desk," said Ms. Denny. "I want you to imagine you're me. You're the teacher."

"Okay," said Lucy uncertainly.

She imagined everyone sitting in their seats. She imagined teaching them new words and organizing craft time. She imagined sending Jacinta to the Time Out chair.

"Now," said Ms. Denny, "tell me what you see."

"Chairs," said Lucy. "Tables, pencils."

"What else?" said Ms. Denny.

"Windows, lights."

"That's right," said Ms. Denny. "Here, have a peppermint."

Lucy reached into the tin and took one. Now she really did feel like Ms. Denny.

"Anything else?"

Lucy peered at the back wall, sucking slowly. The peppermint was very strong and made her eyes water.

"I can see my camel picture," said Lucy. She paused for a moment to consider this. "Ohhh, I get it. *You* can see my camel picture when you're standing here teaching us. You like my drawing!"

Ms. Denny nodded, and Lucy sat up a little straighter. When the bell rang, she stood up.

"Before you go back to your seat," said Ms. Denny, "just so you know, I don't think you're a bad person, Lucy. I think you're rather a character, but that's quite a different thing."

Lucy smiled to herself, a wide grin that lit up her

face. Yesterday had been a Bad day but today, she thought, today was shaping up to be quite a Good one.

And that made sense. She was, after all, Lucy the Good.

GLOSSARY OF
DUTCH WORDS

DANK JE WEL *(dahnk yay vell)*: thank you

GOED SO *(khood sew)*: good

JA *(yah)*: yes

LEKKER *(leck-er)*: yummy

NEE *(nay)*: no

NIET *(neet)*: not

PRACHTIG *(prakh-tikh)*: great, fantastic

SINTERKLAAS *(sin-ter-clahs)*: the Dutch
version of Santa Claus or Saint Nicholas

SPECULAAS *(spek-you-lahs)*: a delicious Dutch
spiced cookie

TANTE *(tahn-teh)*: aunt

ZWARTE PIET *(tsvahr-teh peet)*: Black Piet,
Sinterklaas's helper

SPECULAAS

Ask an adult to help you make these delicious Dutch spiced cookies. This is an old family recipe translated from the cookbook of my aunt Maartje Bijl.

INGREDIENTS

¾ cup all-purpose flour
⅓ cup dark brown sugar
1½ teaspoons baking powder
a pinch of salt
1½ teaspoons ground cinnamon
¼ teaspoon ground cloves
½ teaspoon ground nutmeg
5 tablespoons unsalted butter
1½ to 2 tablespoons milk (or more, if needed)
slivered almonds (optional)

METHOD 1 *(if you have a* speculaas *mold)*

Preheat oven to 325°F. Flour *speculaas* mold. Sift flour, sugar, baking powder, salt, and spices together. Add butter and rub into flour mixture (with your fingers) until it looks like bread crumbs. Add milk. Knead ingredients together to form a firm dough. Add more milk if too dry or more flour if too moist. Chill in fridge for at least half an hour. Press the dough into the mold. Drag a knife across the top to remove excess dough. Tip the mold over and bang it on the back till the dough pops out. Repeat until you have used all the dough. Lay the cookies on a greased baking tray. Add slivered almonds on top (optional). Bake for 15 to 20 minutes (sometimes less, depending on your oven) or until golden brown.

METHOD 2 *(if you don't have a* speculaas *mold)*

Follow the instructions above but instead of pressing the dough into the mold, roll it out until it is about ¼ inch thick. Use cookie cutters to make different shapes. Press almonds into the top of the dough (optional). Bake as above.

Lucy's friends and family tell her about how they deal with their anger, and Lucy comes up with her own solution. What do you do when you're angry? How can you let it out in a good way?

_____

_____

_____

_____

_____

_____

_____

_____

_____

_____

_____

_____

_____

_____

_____

_____

Remember! If this book does not belong to you, you can do this activity on a separate sheet of paper.

ACKNOWLEDGMENTS

I'd like to thank my family and friends for continuing to support and encourage me in my writing endeavors; my publisher, Zoe Walton, and the rest of the team at Random House Australia, for putting in a huge effort and being so enthusiastic about this project; Sheila Drummond, my agent, for her support and for looking after all the negotiations and contractual stuff that pretty much goes over my head; Cheryl Orsini, for her lively illustrations that perfectly capture Lucy's character; everyone who critiqued my manuscript and bolstered me up when I was going through the "my novel is no good and I'll never be published again!" phase, namely, my mum, Russell Talbot, Lyn Eggins, Kate Thorne, and my great online critique group, Critters (Kesta Fleming, Richard Brookton, and Julie Thorndyke); the South Australian Writers' Centre and the Ekidnas group, for being such useful resources and support; Aunty Jenny, for testing the *speculaas* recipe; the Broadview taste-testers, for being culinary guinea pigs; and, finally, the Macquarie Group Foundation LongLines Program, which involved an over-the-phone mentorship with Peter Bishop, Creative Director of Varuna Writers' House, that, despite taking place during the middle of a thunderstorm, was extremely useful and gave rise to the scene featuring Apricot the chicken in the backyard bathtub.